First American Edition.
Copyright © 1998 Disney Enterprises, Inc.
All rights reserved under international copyright conventions.
Published in the United States by Grolier Enterprises Inc.,
Danbury, Connecticut. Originally published in Denmark by
Egmont Gruppen, Copenhagen.

ISBN: 0-7172-8813-7

Manufactured in the United States of America.
A B C D   1 2 3 4

Walt Disney's
Donald Duck's
BIRTHDAY SURPRISE

GROLIER
BOOK CLUB EDITION

"What a great day!" cried Donald Duck one summer morning. The birds were singing and the sun was shining.

But that wasn't the only reason Donald was happy. Today was his birthday!

Donald stretched.
"I think I'll stay in bed
a few more minutes,"
he thought. "After all,
it's my birthday!" He
snuggled under the
covers once more.

"Besides, I'm sure my nephews are
making me a special breakfast."

Donald didn't stay in bed
for long. He didn't want to
keep Huey, Dewey, and
Louie waiting.

But the only thing
waiting for him was a
note on the table downstairs.

Donald read the note.

Dear Uncle Donald,
We've gone out
with our friends.
See you later.

Love,
Huey, Dewey,
and Louie.

"They must have forgotten that today is my birthday," Donald said sadly. He had hoped to find his nephews with a pile of birthday pancakes—and a pile of presents, too!

Then Donald
had an idea. He
ran out of the
house and
jumped into
his car.

"I know
someone who
will remember
my birthday!"
he cried.

Donald's car bounced down the street. He was on his way to Daisy Duck's house.

Donald knocked
on Daisy's door.
There was no answer.

He looked through
a window but didn't
see anyone. "Where
could she be?" he
wondered.

Just then, Clarabelle
Cow called to him.
"Yoo-hoo! Donald!"

Clarabelle told
Donald that Daisy
had gone out that
morning with
Gladstone Gander.

"Gladstone Gander!"
Donald cried jealously.
This was not the
birthday he had
dreamed of!

Donald jumped back in his car. "Hmmph!" he said. "I'll just go and find my cousin Gus Goose! He'll remember that today's my birthday! I bet Gus is planning a surprise party for me right now."

But instead of
finding a party at
the farm, Donald
just found chickens!

"Gus!" he called
out to his cousin.
"Where are you?"

"Try the barn,"
suggested the pigs.

"What an excellent place for a party," Donald thought as he hurried to the barn. But instead of a party, Donald found his cousin Gus napping on a haystack.

"Gus! Wake up! It's me!" Donald cried. But Gus just rolled over and went on snoring.

Donald couldn't believe it. No one had remembered his birthday!

Donald's shoulders sagged as he went back to his car. "Uncle Scrooge McDuck might remember," he said to himself.

But as his car bounced down the road, Donald wasn't sure Uncle Scrooge would even have a card for him, let alone a present.

Soon Donald parked his car outside
of Uncle Scrooge's money bin.

As soon as Donald reached the door, bells started ringing and cameras snapped his picture. Uncle Scrooge had all kinds of alarms and locks to keep his money safe.

"It's only me!" Donald shouted.

Uncle Scrooge's butler looked at Donald through a camera.

"Your uncle is busy counting his money," he told Donald through a loudspeaker. "He cannot be disturbed."

Poor Donald!

"Where is everyone today?" he shouted.

Then he had another idea.

"Of course!" chuckled Donald, as his car sped away from Uncle Scrooge's vault. "Gyro Gearloose will be glad to see me today. He's probably waiting for me right now!"

Donald didn't even have to knock on Gyro's
door. A robot opened it and handed Donald a note.
"I'm trying out my latest flying invention,"
Donald read out loud. "Hope for the best! Gyro."

"I give up!" Donald said with a sigh. He got into his car and slowly drove home.

When Donald finally got home it was dark.
"My birthday is almost over, and no one
remembered," Donald thought with a sniffle.

"I'll just go to bed," said Donald as he walked into his dark house.

"SURPRISE!"

Donald jumped. The lights flashed on and suddenly all his friends began to sing "Happy Birthday."

"You remembered!" Donald gasped.

Daisy and Gladstone, Gyro and Gus,
Clarabelle, Grandma Duck, Uncle Scrooge,
Huey, Dewey, and Louie—all of Donald's
friends were there.

"Happy birthday, Donald!" they cried.

"Come and open your presents,
Uncle Donald," cried Huey,
Dewey, and Louie.

"Presents? Oh, boy!"
said Donald with a laugh.

"Blow out the candles on
your cake, first," said Daisy.
"Grandma and I have been
baking all day!"

"Oh, Donald—I made you a shirt,"
said Grandma Duck.

She held out the shirt for Donald
to try on.

"Thanks, Grandma," Donald said.
"I love the color blue!"

"And here's a little something for your piggy bank," Uncle Scrooge said as he handed Donald a gold coin.

Daisy winked at Donald.
"You get more handsome every
year," she told him. Donald blushed.

Gladstone gave Donald an envelope. "There are two tickets inside to the ball game this weekend," he told Donald.

"Oh, boy!" shouted Donald.

Huey, Dewey, and Louie had even made
a birthday banner for everyone to sign.
"We love you, Uncle Donald," they
wrote on the banner.

"Okay, everyone," called Gyro. "Let's pose together for a picture. Smile!"

Gyro set the camera and hurried over to get into the picture.

FLASH!

"I can't wait to see how it turns out," Donald said happily.

Donald didn't have to wait long. The photo was ready in just a few minutes.

"I'm the lucky duck! Everyone remembered my birthday, after all," Donald thought happily.

"And it has turned out to be the best birthday ever."